John's Choice

by Jane Belk Moncure
illustrated by
Lydia Halverson

Published by The Dandelion House
A Division of The Child's World

Distributed by Scripture Press Publications, Wheaton, Illinois 60187.

Library of Congress Cataloging in Publication Data

Moncure, Jane Belk.
  John's choice.

  Summary: When Mr. Morrow gives John too much money
in change, John considers buying a bag of stick candy
instead of returning the money to the store.
  [1. Honesty—Fiction] I. Halverson, Lydia, ill.
II. Title.
PZ7.M739Jo   [E]   82-7461
ISBN 0-89693-207-9   AACR2

Published by The Dandelion House, A Division of The Child's World, Inc.
© 1982 SP Publications, Inc. All rights reserved. Printed in U.S.A.

1 2 3 4 5 6 7 8 9 10 11 12 R 89 88 87 86 85 84 83 82

John's Choice

"Wow! You've been in the creek again," said John when he saw Bo's muddy tracks all over the porch.

Bo just wagged his tail.

"I'll clean you up before Mom sees all this mud!"

Just then Mom opened the door and Bo bounded inside.

"Catch him!" shouted Mom. "That dog belongs in the barn!"

John pulled. Mom pushed.

"Out you go," she said. "Out! Out!"

"I'll give him a bath right now," said John.

"And clean the porch," added Mom.

John found the washtub by the chicken house, but he couldn't find a bar of soap anywhere.

Mom gave him a fifty-cent piece.

"Run down to Mr. Morrow's store and buy a bar of soap," she said. "Bring back the change, all of it."

John put the money in his pocket. Off he raced with Bo in the lead.

Mr. Morrow's store was about a mile down the sandy road. It was just on the edge of a small town. John knew a short cut. He climbed the pasture fence, ran past the barn and followed a path through the woods.

As John crossed the footbridge over the creek, he saw Bo splashing in the water. Then Bo rolled in the mud!

"Come on Frisky Boy! You're in double trouble." Bo wagged his tail. Soon he dashed after a squirrel.

As John walked along, he reached into his pocket. He wanted to be sure the money was still there. It was.

When they came to the store, John left Bo outside. He knew Mr. Morrow didn't care much for dogs—especially muddy ones.

"Hi, Mr. Morrow," he called. Mr. Morrow was busy putting cans on the shelf. He didn't even turn around. So John looked for the soap. There were boxes, barrels and kegs. There were pots and pans, shoes, and all kinds of things in Mr. Morrow's store. Soon John found the soap. He took a bar of it to the counter.

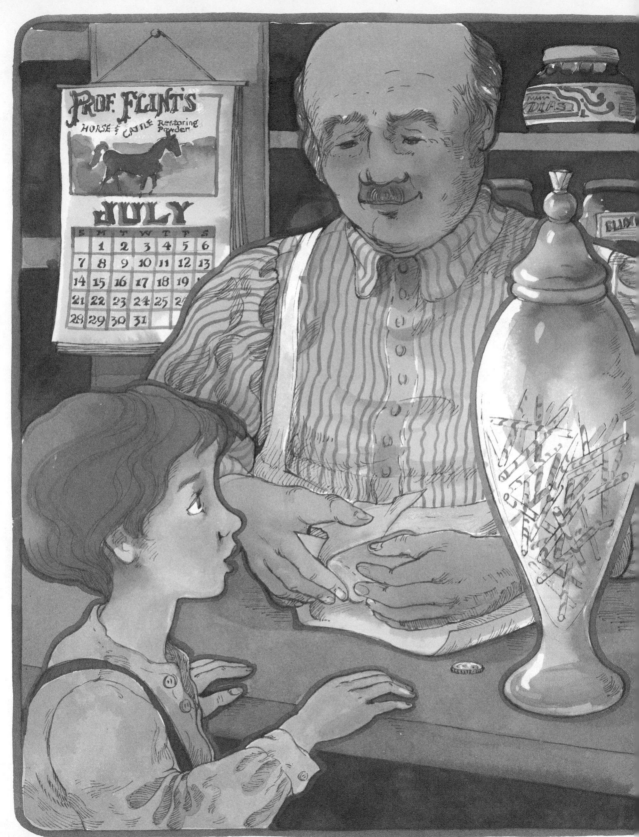

Right by the cash register was a big glass jar of stick candy. John wished for a penny!

John put the money on the counter. "Here's the money for the soap, Mr. Morrow. I'm going to wash my dog."

Mr. Morrow wrapped up the soap.

But, before Mr. Morrow could give John his
change, the telephone rang. John stood there.
Mr. Morrow talked on and on. John waited.
And waited! Finally he said, "Please, Mr.
Morrow! I'm in a hurry!"

Still talking, Mr. Morrow reached over. He took some money out of the cash register and handed it to John. John picked up the soap and hurried out. Only then did he count the money in his hand.

"Let's see—the soap costs ten cents. I gave Mr. Morrow fifty cents. So I should have forty cents." John counted the dimes in his hand. "Ten cents, twenty, thirty, forty, fifty, *Fifty cents!*" he shouted. "Mr. Morrow gave me too much change—ten cents too much!"

BAGPIPE
MATCHES

drink
Orange
Ade

John grinned, and Bo wagged his tail!

"Yipee! I can buy a whole bag of candy sticks." But then John thought, "The money's not really mine." Then, he said aloud, "Nobody else knows."

Next John thought about Mom. He knew right away what she would say. She would say, "Hey wait a minute. That's Mr. Morrow's dime." He knew what Mom would do. She would take it back. John stood there a moment, thinking.

"Yeah," he said to himself, "that's the right thing to do." But then he thought, "*Mom will never know. Nobody knows but me.*"

John put the money in his pocket and started home. But the money felt heavy. Something inside seemed to say, "Take it back."

Then John remembered something. Mr. Morrow might not know about the extra dime. And Mom might not know about it. But God knew.

Slowly, John turned around and went back inside the store. Mr. Morrow was still talking on the telephone. John waited. Finally, he called out, "Mr. Morrow, you gave me the wrong change."

Mr. Morrow leaned over the counter. "Listen, boy," he said sternly, "I don't make mistakes! Now run along home."

John hurried outside again. He stood there wondering what to do.

"Well," John said to himself, "I told Mr. Morrow about the mistake. But he doesn't want to listen. He doesn't know that the mistake was giving me too much change. Maybe it's okay to keep the dime after all." But from deep down inside him, a voice seemed to say, "John, the money isn't yours."

"Help me, Lord," John prayed.

It took courage to open that screen door again. But John did it. He went back inside Mr. Morrow's store.

Without a word, John walked up to the counter. He plunked down the dime.

Looking into Mr. Morrow's surprised face, he said, "Well, it ain't mine." And ran out.

Now he had the bar of soap in his hand and the right change in his pocket.

Bo wasn't too happy. Maybe he knew he was in for a bath. But John felt good all over.